The Charlotte Stories

The

Charlotte Stories

Teddy Jam

WITH ILLUSTRATIONS BY
HARVEY CHAN

A GROUNDWOOD BOOK
DOUGLAS & McINTYRE
TORONTO VANCOUVER BUFFALO

Text copyright © 1994 by Teddy Jam
Illustrations copyright © 1994 by Harvey Chan
First paperback edition 1997

Groundwood Books/Douglas & McIntyre
585 Bloor Street West, Toronto, Ontario M6G 1K5

Distributed in the U.S.A. by Publishers Group West
4065 Hollis Street, Emeryville, CA 94608

We acknowledge the support of the Canada Council for the Arts and the Ontario Arts Council for our publishing program.

Canadian Cataloguing in Publication Data
Jam, Teddy
The Charlotte stories
"A Groundwood Book".
ISBN 0-88899-210-6 (bound) ISBN 0-88899-302-1 (pbk.)
I. Chan, Harvey. II. Title.
PS8569.A427C46   jC813'.54   C94-930725-4
PZ7.J36Ch

Design by Michael Solomon
Printed and bound in Canada

CONTENTS

The New Boy

Charlotte loved hanging upside down. In the park there was a bar where Charlotte could hang from her knees.

"Hanging upside down is going to make you dizzy and fall," Charlotte's father would say.

"Hanging upside down is going to make your teeth confused," Nikki would say.

"Hanging upside down is turning your brain backward," Miriam said.

"I don't care," was Charlotte's reply. People said her brain was in her head but she never felt it thinking.

"Are you supposed to feel your brain thinking?" Charlotte once asked her doctor.

Dr. Clancy laughed. Charlotte thought she knew why. It was because Dr. Clancy knew Charlotte didn't have a brain but didn't want to make fun of her.

Dr. Clancy always put his stethoscope to Charlotte's heart, looked in

her ears and pressed her tongue down
to peer down her throat. He even
looked at her eyes with a special funny
light. But he never did anything about
Charlotte's brain.

One day Charlotte's teacher took the class to the museum to see dinosaur skeletons. The teacher pointed to their heads and said, "That's where their brains were." Then she explained to the children that dinosaurs had big bodies and small brains. Unlike children who had small bodies and big brains.

"Though you wouldn't always believe it," the teacher said.

Hanging upside down, Charlotte

watched Miriam on the swing beside her. Miriam was eating half a popsicle. So was Charlotte. Miriam's father bought them just one popsicle at a time, from the store across the street, and they split it. That way Charlotte didn't have to eat a whole popsicle upside down.

"Your face is turning red," Miriam said.

"Not as red as him," said Charlotte, pointing at a boy who was just coming into the park.

She had seen the boy before but didn't know his name. Even though it was summer he was wearing a complete hockey uniform: a red Montreal Canadiens' sweater, long matching socks, shorts over the socks, pads that made everything bulge. In his hand he carried a stick, a helmet and a tennis ball.

When he got near the brick wall of the public bathroom he put on his helmet. Then he started banging the tennis ball against the wall.

"There he goes again. When he grows up he's going to be an animal," Miriam said.

"What kind of animal?"

"The kind of animal that plays sports all the time, stupid. Like those boys who always play football out on

the street. One day they're going to get run over, though they probably won't even notice, they're so dumb."

"Oh," said Charlotte.

"My sister Kelly used to go out with a boy like that," Miriam explained. "She called him Benny-the-Lunk."

"I remember Benny," Charlotte said. "He made Kelly cry."

Charlotte also remembered that, but she didn't say anything. Kelly was ten years older than Miriam. She let Charlotte and Miriam come into her room and play with her makeup and do their hair with her. Sometimes when Charlotte slept over at Miriam's, Kelly gave them their baths, then washed their hair for them, putting it into funny shapes with rollers and ribbons.

The boy was standing in front of Charlotte. She was thinking that her head was starting to get hot and that maybe she would come down for a while.

"Do you want to play?" the boy asked.

His face looked funny upside down. He was wearing his helmet and sweat was coming out.

"No thanks," Miriam said.

Charlotte had been about to say yes.

The boy stepped closer to Charlotte. The closer he got, the funnier he looked.

"Don't touch me," Charlotte said.

"I wasn't going to," said the boy. "I was going to help you down."

"I don't need help," Charlotte said. "Out of the way." Then she swung down. She knew her face was red and sweaty.

"We were talking about something," said Miriam. "Go away."

The boy backed up a step.

Charlotte looked at Miriam. Miriam pushed back her hair the way she always did when she was pretending to be angry, the way her sister Kelly did when she was talking about Benny-the-Lunk.

Charlotte pushed back her hair.

She remembered the time she had been at Miriam's, Kelly taking care of them, and then Kelly had looked out the window at the boys playing football and said they were all lunks. Just like

Benny. Then her nose went red and her eyes squinched and she reached for some kleenex.

After, Miriam said that Kelly had been crying.

"My father does that," Charlotte said. Not crying, she meant, but squinching his eyes and reaching for kleenex. Then he would sneeze, especially in the spring and fall. That was also his excuse for not letting Charlotte have a cat, like Miriam did, or a dog, which was what Charlotte really wanted.

The next time they went to the park it was Charlotte's mother's turn to take them. The boy, dressed in his hockey uniform, was banging the tennis ball against the brick bathroom wall.

Charlotte watched him while she hung upside down.

When the boy asked them to play, Charlotte said yes, quickly, before Miriam could say no.

"No," Miriam said. But it was too late.

Charlotte got down. The boy dropped the ball. Charlotte picked it up. Then she threw it. She had meant to throw it against the bathroom wall so it would bounce back but she missed and it went over by the slides. She ran to get it. The boy ran after her but

Charlotte got there first. When she saw the boy coming at her she threw the ball to Miriam. Miriam threw the ball back to her but the boy caught it. The three of them played monkey-in-the-middle until Charlotte's mother made them go home.

Later that afternoon the boy appeared while the girls were playing in Miriam's backyard. He stood in the laneway, still wearing his hockey clothes, and looked over the fence at them.

"Can I play?"

"We're not playing," Miriam said. "We're talking."

The boy held up a bag and showed them some chocolate bars. "All right," said Miriam, "you can come and play. Climb over the fence."

He had a tennis ball in his pocket and they played baseball with a stick until supper time.

"He's a lunk," Miriam said later. It was her turn to sleep at Charlotte's house. "He just brought those chocolate bars so he could play with us."

"I don't care," Charlotte said.

"I don't care either," said Miriam. "I guess he can play as long as he brings presents."

"He shouldn't need to bring presents," Charlotte's mother said. "You should let him play with you whenever he wants to."

"Do we have to?" Charlotte asked.

"Why not? He seems like a nice boy."

"I don't like playing with boys," Miriam said. "I don't have to if I don't want to."

"Don't you want to?"

Miriam shrugged, then turned to Charlotte. "Let's watch television," she said.

The next day when the boy was climbing over the fence he ripped his hockey sweater. He started to cry.

"What's wrong?" Charlotte asked.

"My father is going to kill me for this—"

"I can fix it," Miriam said.

She ran upstairs and came down with her doll sewing kit.

"You have to take your sweater off," said Miriam. "I don't want to stab you."

She sent Charlotte into the house to get some glasses of water while she worked.

When Charlotte came back she gave everyone their drinks.

"His name is Patrick," Miriam said.

"Just like Patrick Roy the hockey player," the boy said. "That's what I'm going to be."

He put on his helmet. Then he climbed the fence and went home.

That night, after her parents kissed her goodnight, Charlotte closed her eyes. She got a picture of herself hanging upside down. She was at the park and the boy, wearing his uniform and his helmet, was banging the tennis ball

against the bathroom wall. She wondered what it would be like to be in the bathroom with the tennis ball crashing against the wall. Then she wondered what it would be like to be a brain inside a head inside a helmet.

That must be why people wore helmets, to protect their brains.

She wondered if the boy ever felt his brain thinking. She decided to ask him the next day.

The Birthday Party

A week before Charlotte's birthday, her mother asked who she wanted to invite to the party.

"I don't want a party," Charlotte said.

"Of course you want a party. Miriam will come. And how about inviting Laura? You and Laura always play together at school."

"I don't want to invite Laura.

Yesterday she wouldn't share the red paint."

"That was just a mistake," Charlotte's mother said. "How about Sarah-Jane? You have to invite Sarah-Jane. You went to her party, remember?"

"I don't like Sarah-Jane anymore. She only invited me because I said I would give her a present if she did."

"Everyone gives presents at birthday parties."

"I know that," Charlotte said.

"Nikki would be a good person to

ask. You like Nikki. Remember that time he put a bandage on your knee after he kicked you?"

"Nikki smells funny," Charlotte said.

"That's a terrible thing to say. How would you like it if Nikki said you smelled funny?"

"He told me that my mouth smelled like peanut butter and I didn't like it."

"See?"

"Then I kicked him and I didn't give him a bandage. He cried."

"That was mean," Charlotte's mother said.

"I know. But it wasn't my fault. He made me."

"No one ever makes you kick them. No wonder you don't have any friends."

"No wonder I don't want a party!"

Charlotte shouted. Then she started crying and ran upstairs.

The day of Charlotte's party the sun came out for the first time in two weeks. Charlotte's mother had tied ribbons and balloons all over the house. In the morning Charlotte's father set up the barbecue and went downtown to buy special hot dogs and three kinds of ice cream.

For the party Charlotte wore her favorite pink dress with pleats on the front and a white bow that tied around her back. Before the guests came her father took her picture. "Smile," he said. "You look just like a little princess."

"I don't feel like a little princess,"

Charlotte said. "I hope no one comes to my party."

"Don't be silly," her father said. "You're just feeling funny because it's your birthday. When I was a little boy I used to hate my birthday, too. One time I hid in the cupboard and pretended I was kidnapped."

"What happened?" Charlotte asked.

"No one knew I was pretending."

"I'm not going to hide in the cupboard," said Charlotte. "Yesterday in kindergarten Nikki hid in the cupboard and a spider bit him on the ear."

"You could hide somewhere else," her father said.

"I don't want to hide," Charlotte said. "You can hide if you want to. The way you did last year during my party, remember? Mommy said you hid downstairs and watched television the whole time and she had to blow up all the balloons."

"Don't be silly," Charlotte's father said. "I would never hide on your birthday. I was just watching a very

important football game. It was over by the time the other parents came."

The first guest to arrive was Sarah-Jane. She was wearing a pink dress with a white bow around its back.

"Look at you," Charlotte's father

said. "You look just like a princess."

"I know," Sarah-Jane said. She reached into her bag and took out a crown. "I am a princess."

"No you're not," Charlotte said.

"Yes I am. Your father told me and so did mine."

"Great!" Charlotte said. She went upstairs and closed the door to her room. People came and knocked on it but she called out, "Look at my sign if you can read. If you can't, I'll tell you what it says. Do Not Disturb!"

Charlotte's mother came to the door.

"It's your birthday, dear," she said. "All your friends are here."

"I know," Charlotte said. "I can see them and I can hear them and I can smell them."

"That's a terrible thing to say," Charlotte's mother said.

"That's right," said Charlotte. "I am a terrible little girl and I wish it wasn't my birthday." From her window she could see the other children playing in the backyard. They were all shouting and laughing and playing tag with each other. Even Nikki, who was the only boy except for Patrick who was wearing his hockey sweater and Alexander who was Mary's little brother and had to come or else he would cry for a week. At least, that's what Mary's mother said. She was in the backyard, too,

helping with the children and lighting
the barbecue for the hot dogs.

"Is something bothering you?"
Charlotte's mother asked.

"You are," Charlotte said.

"It's your birthday," Charlotte's
mother said. "I don't think you're
behaving very well."

"You behave," Charlotte said. "Can't
you read the sign on my door?"

"Excuse me," said her mother. She
came into Charlotte's room. Charlotte
had changed out of her party dress and

was wearing her ballet costume.

"You're a funny little girl," Charlotte's mother said.

"No I'm not."

"Is anything wrong?"

"Yes," Charlotte said. Her mother was sitting on the bed. She climbed onto her mother's lap. She closed her eyes. When she closed her eyes she saw what she had been seeing every night

for a week. When she closed her eyes she saw darkness, darkness filled with strange smells, the same darkness she had seen at the daycare when they had started playing hide-and-seek and she had shut herself in the cleaning cupboard so no one would find her.

At first it was fun and she could hear the others running around. Then the smells of the old rags made her feel sick and she was sure she could feel spiders crawling on her. She tried to get out of the cupboard but the handle was stuck. She wanted to scream but she thought

everyone would laugh at her if she did because the other day Nikki had called her a crybaby when she said she was afraid of spiders.

She tried the handle again. Then she pushed the door as hard as she could.

The door flew open and she stumbled out. Nikki and Sarah-Jane were on the other side, looking at her.

"You smell funny," Nikki said.

"No she doesn't," said Sarah-Jane, but Charlotte was already running away from them, out into the playroom.

"So that's why you didn't want your birthday party," Charlotte's mother said.

Charlotte nodded. Although now, looking out the back window, she didn't mind seeing all her friends in the backyard.

When she went downstairs no one

said anything about her ballet suit.
Soon they all went into the kitchen and
Charlotte had to close her eyes while
the cake was brought in and everyone
sang Happy Birthday. When she closed
her eyes this time, Charlotte didn't see
how it had been inside the cupboard.
Instead she just felt tired, as though it
was already night and she was lying in
bed listening to her parents.

When it was time for her to cut the cake Nikki sat beside her. She edged away from him but he pressed his shoulder against hers and when she turned to tell him to go away he gave her such a big smile that she didn't bother.

She gave the first and the biggest piece to Sarah-Jane. The next went to Nikki. Soon everyone was eating cake and ice cream and Charlotte was listening to Nikki tell Emily that he knew how to swim and was going to go fishing with his father.

Charlotte felt happy enough to cry, but she didn't. She gave herself a second piece of cake. After all, it was her birthday party.

Charlotte and the Mouse

One Saturday morning Charlotte was
sitting in the kitchen with her mother.
The sun was coming through the window
at a funny slant and Charlotte could see
the little pieces of dust dancing in the
light. She wondered what would happen
if a fly flew through that dust. Probably
it would get knocked down, Charlotte
decided.

"Charlotte, how many times do I have to ask you? Do you want some toast?"

"You don't ever have to ask me," Charlotte replied. "You know I always want toast. Toast with honey and margarine, please."

It was a weekend. On weekends she could have toast with honey and margarine but during the week she could only have cold cereal and milk because her mother had to rush to drop her at the daycare before work.

"I'll have twelve pieces," Charlotte said. "One for each month."

Her mother went to the breadbox. She was wearing the pink housecoat

Charlotte and her father had given her for Christmas. It was covered with dancing red elephants.

"You've got elephants on your bum," Charlotte said, as though for the first time.

"AAAAH!" shrieked her mother. She jumped backward and fell onto the floor.

"I was only kidding," said Charlotte. "They're just pictures of elephants."

Her mother had scrambled to her feet and slammed the breadbox shut. "CHARLES!" she screamed. Then she turned to Charlotte. "Don't open that box. It's got a mouse in it."

"It does?" Charlotte went and put her hand on the breadbox. She could hear the mouse scrabbling around inside.

"Can I see it?"

"Don't let it in the kitchen," said her mother.

"Don't let what in the kitchen?" Charlotte's father asked.

"The mouse," Charlotte said. "It's in the breadbox."

Charlotte's mother stood up and dusted off her elephants.

They all listened to the mouse trying
to get out.

"I bet there's about ten of them,"
Charlotte said.

"Do something," Charlotte's mother
said. Then she looked at Charlotte.
"I'm not really afraid of that mouse. I'm
just pretending."

Charlotte's father slid open the lid of
the breadbox. The mouse sounds got

louder. Charlotte looked in. She could see a loaf of bread sticking up. A little square had been eaten out of the corner of each slice. "I thought mice only liked cheese," Charlotte said.

Her father closed the lid, then he took the box outside.

Charlotte followed him. "What are you going to do?"

"I'm going to let the mouse go," her father said.

Next door Miriam was outside with her father. He was digging in the garden. She came over to talk to Charlotte.

"We have a mouse," Charlotte said.

"We had one last week but it got away."

Charlotte's father's bare feet looked funny in the wet grass. Miriam's father was wearing rubber boots. So was Miriam. Charlotte was wearing her mother's gray slippers. They looked like bunnies.

Charlotte's father opened the breadbox. All the bread spilled out. The

mouse ran through the grass and hid in the bushes.

That afternoon, while her mother was shopping and her father was upstairs fixing the storm windows, Charlotte opened the back door. Then she made a little trail of cheese crumbs from the backyard into the kitchen. For a long time she waited to see if the mouse would come. She remembered her mother saying, "A watched pot never boils," so, leaving the door open, she went upstairs to watch her father.

During supper there was a scrabbling sound again. This time it was in one of the cupboards.

"Listen," said Charlotte's mother. "It's that mouse again."

"You're lucky," said Miriam. She was on a sleepover at Charlotte's. "Our mouse got away and never came back."

"I'm putting out that mousetrap

tonight!" said Charlotte's mother.

"That's what my parents did," Miriam said.

"No," Charlotte protested.

"We'll talk about it later."

Later, when Charlotte and Miriam were lying in Charlotte's room, supposed to be asleep in the dark, Miriam said, "Your mother never talked about that trap."

"We know what that means," Charlotte said.

"Poor mouse," sighed Miriam.

"We could set my alarm," said Charlotte. "Then, after my parents go to sleep..."

They set Charlotte's alarm and put it under the mattress.

When they woke up it was the middle of the night.

"Are you awake?" Charlotte whispered to Miriam.

"Sssh. Let's go downstairs."

Carefully they opened Charlotte's door. The nightlight from the bathroom shone a thin hollow light onto the stairs. Slowly they crept down.

They turned on the kitchen light.

In front of the stove was a huge mousetrap. It was baited with a piece of cheese.

"I knew they liked cheese," Charlotte said.

"Go away mouse," whispered Miriam.

"I know what," Charlotte said. "We could stay here all night in case the mouse comes out to the trap."

"We could give it some other cheese instead."

Miriam opened the refrigerator. Charlotte took out some cheese. They cut up some lumps and put them on a plate in the middle of the floor.

"I'll show you a trick," Miriam said. She took a knife and stuck it into the trap. The trap jumped up into the air, turned several somersaults, then landed on the floor with a bang.

"Shhh!" they both hissed.

Then they put the plate of cheese in a cupboard, turned off all the lights and crept back to bed.

In the morning Charlotte's mother looked at the sprung trap. "Those mice," she said. "Are we trapping them or feeding them?"

Every evening at supper Charlotte would hear the mouse somewhere in the kitchen. Then her mother, after the dishes were done, would set the trap. That was the deal between Charlotte's parents. Her mother would set the trap but, when the mouse got caught, her father would get rid of it. They didn't discuss this in front of Charlotte but Charlotte heard them talking about it while she was in the bath.

Every night Charlotte would set her alarm, go downstairs and spring the trap with a knife, the way Miriam had shown her. Then she would put some cheese crumbs on the counter.

In the morning her mother would come down and the trap would be sprung. Charlotte would look on the counter and see that the cheese crumbs had been eaten. "Good mouse," she would say, but very softly.

She began telling the other kids in her class that she had a pet mouse. One of the kids told the teacher and then the teacher asked her if it was true. "It might be a secret," Charlotte said.

That evening, when her mother picked her up, Charlotte's teacher said she'd heard Charlotte was keeping a mouse as a pet. Charlotte's mother laughed.

"She must be," she said. "We've been trying to trap it for nights. If the trap

doesn't work tonight I'm going to make
Charles put out poison."

That night when her alarm went off
Charlotte was too tired to get up.
When she woke up in the morning she
realized she'd slept through the alarm.
"Oh no." She jumped out of bed. It was
still early, before anyone got up, and
the sky was just starting to get light.

She ran down to the kitchen. Instead
of turning on the light she just skidded

right across the floor to the trap. It was empty. Then she had a funny feeling. As though someone was watching her. Someone who had been watching her every single night. She turned around.

On the counter was the mouse, sitting and looking at her. It had its head cocked to one side, like a dog. "You look like a dog," Charlotte thought but didn't say, because she didn't want to scare it.

The mouse's small dark eyes darted about the room. Its legs were trembling. "You don't have to worry," Charlotte said. "It's just me."

The mouse didn't move. Upstairs the toilet flushed. Soon her father would be downstairs. He would see the trap without a mouse inside. And then he would put out poison.

Charlotte opened the back door. "Go," she said to the mouse.

It was cold outside. Through the door Charlotte could see the grass had turned white with frost.

"Go, hurry up. I promise if you go I'll put food out for you every night."

The mouse didn't move.

Charlotte opened the refrigerator and took out the cheese. She made a little trail of crumbs from the door and

down the steps to the backyard. It was
so cold the wood felt like ice against her
bare feet.

"Go," Charlotte begged. "Please go."

She could hear her father starting
down the stairs.

"I'll take you," Charlotte said. She
cupped her hands and walked toward
the mouse, trying not to think about
how the mouse's scratchy little feet and
cold little nose were going to feel when

she picked it up. But just as she reached out, the mouse took a tremendous leap from the counter to the floor—probably setting a world mouse-jump record—skidded halfway across the room and ran outside.

Charlotte closed the door. When she turned around, her father was standing in the kitchen.

He turned on the light, then took a knife from the drawer and handed it to Charlotte. "Better take care of that trap," he said. Charlotte stuck the knife into the trap. It jumped up in the air, turned three somersaults and landed with a loud bang.

"Perfect," said her father. "An

Olympic mouse deserves an Olympic mouse trap." He picked up the trap and threw it in the garbage. Then he scooped the cheese crumbs from the floor, opened the back door and tossed them outside.

"Am I in trouble?" Charlotte asked.

"No," said her father. "You want a ride?" He picked Charlotte up and carried her across the kitchen to the cereal cupboard. "What'll it be?"

"Mouseflakes," Charlotte said, giggling.

She was still eating when her mother came into the kitchen.

"Mission accomplished," said Charlotte's father.

"Did you—?"

"Ask Charlotte."

Her mother turned to Charlotte. She was wearing her elephant housecoat

over her dress so it wouldn't get dirty for work.

"It got away," Charlotte said, pointing at the door.

"Great," said her mother. "What'll it be for lunch, peanut butter or cheese?" She went to the breadbox and leaned over it.

"You've got elephants on your bum," Charlotte said, as though for the first time.

"AAAAAH!" shrieked her mother. She jumped backward and fell onto the floor.

Charlotte came rushing over.

"Just kidding," her mother said calmly, getting up. "It was only an elephant."